W9-AZB-972

MOONJINMEDIA

Reprinted and Distributed by Creative Teaching Press 2013

First Published March, 2011

Published by Moonjinmedia Co., Ltd.

www.moonjin.com

Text © 2011 Moonjinmedia Co.,Ltd.

Illustrations © 2011 Yoonju Kang

All rights reserved.

No part of this publication may be reproduced,
stored in or introduced into a retrieval system,
or transmitted in any form, or by any means
(electronic, mechanical, photocopying, recording or otherwise)
without the prior written permission of the publisher.

ISBN 978-89-539-3480-1

e-CIP Homepage
http://www.nl.go.kr/cip.php
CIP: CIP2011000204

I'm a Little Teapot

Rozanne Lanczak Williams / Yoonju Kang

I'm a little teapot, short and stout.

Here is my handle, here is my spout.

When I get all steamed up, hear me shout,

Tip me over and pour me out!

Here are the teacups, two by two.

Yellow cups, green cups, purple and blue.

We put them on the saucers, one by one.

We will have a party, we will have fun!

Here are the little spoons, all in a line.

We're getting ready for a very fun time!

Put down the napkins, one for each guest.

Let's finish this and take a little rest.

Here are the cookies on a pretty plate.

Hurry! Hurry! Don't be late!

Let's blow up balloons and tie them to chairs.

Let's put pretty flowers everywhere!

Here are some fruits, they're juicy and sweet.

Fruits are yummy party treats!

Apples and bananas, melons and grapes.

Fruits in many colors, fruits in many shapes.

Our table is ready, our friends are coming in.

Hello! Hello! Let's begin!

Pour the tea, pass the treats, we're glad you're all here.

Nothing is better than having friends near.

Here are the cupcakes on a fancy dish.

We can light the candles and you can make a wish.

I wish for happy times for all my friends.

I wish our happy times will never end!